Len Lucero and Kristina Tracy

How to Roll Like Chris P. Bacon

illustrated by Penny Weber

HAY HOUSE, INC.
Carlsbad, California · New York City
London · Sydney · Johannesburg
Vancouver · Hong Kong · New Delhi

Published and distributed in the United States by: Hay House, Inc.: www.hayhouse.com® • **Published and distributed in Australia by:** Hay House Australia Pty. Ltd.: www.hayhouse.com .au • **Published and distributed in the United Kingdom by:** Hay House UK, Ltd.: www.hayhouse.co.uk • **Published and distributed in the Republic of South Africa by:** Hay House SA (Pty), Ltd.: www.hayhouse.co.za • **Distributed in Canada by:** Raincoast Books : www.raincoast.com • **Published in India by:** Hay House Publishers India: www.hayhouse.co.in

Editorial assistance and interior design: Jenny Richards • *Illustrations:* © Penny Weber • *Interior photos:* © Len Lucero

Library of Congress Control Number is on file at the Library of Congress

ISBN: 978-1-4019-4440-7

10 9 8 7 6 5 4 3 2 1
1st edition, November 2014

Printed in China

"This book is dedicated to our friends and family. Their unconditional love, understanding, and encouragement is the driving force behind all that we do. Thank you for everything!"

—Len Lucero

Hi! Remember me? My name is Chris P. Bacon, and I happen to be a very yoooo-neek pig (and also a very loved pig!). Some of you may know me from my first book, *Chris P. Bacon...My Life So Far.* Or maybe you recognize me from my popular YouTube video or from TV. Just in case you missed any of that, let's check out some special memories from my first year.

I was adopted when I was just a little piglet by the nicest man ever (he's a veterinarian, too!) and his family.

Me and Dr. Len (Dad!)

My welcome home party

I am very yoooo-neek because my back legs don't work like most pigs. But, lucky me! My dad made me a special cart to help me get around. A funny video of me learning to use my cart got pretty popular on YouTube, and after that I got to be on TV and visit lots of fun places and meet nice people.

Learning to use my cart... whoaaaa!

That was a couple years ago, and since then I have been rolling nonstop! Along the way I've made many friends and learned a few things about life.

Slippery fun!

Making friends

I wrote this book to share some of the things I have learned that I think are most important, not just for pigs and kids but for everyone! So, here we go . . . !

Be Adventurous!

You don't always need to keep
your feet on the ground.

When you take a leap of faith,
adventure can be found.

Let your fears fall away;
be daring and bold.

When the chance comes along—
go ahead, grab ahold!

Get Silly!

Life is supposed to
be fun, you know.

So don't be afraid to
let your silly side show.

When it's time to get goofy,
no need to be shy.

Just grab a bucket,
and give it a try!

Maybe you wore the
wrong clothes, like me.

Or perhaps you weren't looking
and ran into a tree.

Embarassing moments do happen,
so here's my advice...

Just smile, shake it off, and
don't think about it twice.

Pitch In!

In my family there's
always something to do.

And I would guess it's
the same in yours, too.

When you're part of a family
there's always work to be done.

Pitch in where you can—
you might even have fun!

A smile is something
that is easy to do.

Share yours with another,
and they'll be smiling, too!

When you pass one along,
you can make someone's day.

And you don't even have to go
out of your way!

When I was a piglet
some things made me scared.

But I've learned that they're not
as bad as I feared.

When you feel like there's
something that you can't do,

Just step up and over
and push bravely through.

Whether you're building a fort
or making a treat,

Doing stuff with friends
can't be beat.

We all have a blast when we're
hanging out together,

And when we are done we have
a day to remember.

Be Generous!

I love to be generous
whenever I can,

Whether it's buying my pals ice cream
or lending a hand.

When I give to others
I feel as happy as can be.

It seems the more I give
the more good comes back to me.

We all love to share
exciting news—it's fun—

But gossip can really
hurt someone.

So when you want to spread a story,
here's what you do:

Ask yourself if you would tell it,
if it were about you.

yoooo-neek, Like Me!

You may not have your own wheels
or feathers and a beak,

But I'll bet you have something
that makes you yoooo-neek.

Be proud of how you're different
and you will find out,

That loving your yoooo-neekness
is what it's all about!

Well, I hope you enjoyed learning how to roll like me! Before I say good-bye, I have one more thing to share with you. This is one of my favorite recipes! Gather up some friends—furry, feathered, or human (find an adult to help you)—and make these delicious cookies called Pigs in Mud!
Yuuum-eeeee!

PIGS IN MUD

Ingredients

3 sticks salted butter at room temperature
1 cup sugar
1 teaspoon vanilla extract
3½ cups all-purpose flour
1 cup semisweet chocolate chips

Get a big bowl and mix together the butter and sugar. Add the vanilla and stir. Then add the flour. Mix it all up until you have a nice ball of dough. (You can use a spoon or an electric mixer or even your hands!) Once it is mixed, cover the bowl of dough in plastic wrap and put it in the fridge for half an hour. When you take the dough out of the fridge, put it on a floured surface and make it into a big pancake shape.

Find a rolling pin and roll the dough out until it's ¼-inch thick. Preheat the oven to 350 degrees. Use your pig cookie cutter (or another shape if you must) to cut out the cookies. Place your cut-out pigs on an ungreased baking sheet. Bake until they are just golden brown around the edges (about 14-16 minutes). Take the cookies out of the oven and let them cool.

Now for the delicious chocolate! Melt the chocolate chips in the microwave or in a pan on the stove. When the chocolate is nice and smooth, dip the pigs' legs and tummies into the mud. (I mean chocolate, dip the pigs' legs and tummies And here comes the best part...eat them!!

SOME NEW
PICS OF ME...

I love my dad!

Hello, goat!

Selfie

Sniffin'

Snack time!!

THE FUN NEVER ENDS!

Me and Aspen on the lookout

Chillin' by the pool

Me on TV!

My favorite book!

We hope you enjoyed this Hay House book. If you'd like to receive our online catalog featuring additional information on Hay House books and products, or if you'd like to find out more about the Hay Foundation, please contact:

Hay House, Inc.
P.O. Box 5100
Carlsbad, CA 92018-5100

(760) 431-7695 or (800) 654-5126
(760) 431-6948 (fax) or (800) 650-5115 (fax)
www.hayhouse.com® · www.hayfoundation.org

Published and distributed in Australia by: Hay House Australia Pty. Ltd., 18/36 Ralph St., Alexandria NSW 2015
Phone: 612-9669-4299 · Fax: 612-9669-4144 · www.hayhouse.com.au

Published and distributed in the United Kingdom by: Hay House UK, Ltd., Astley House, 33 Notting Hill Gate, London W11 3JQ
Phone: 44-20-3675-2450 · Fax: 44-20-3675-2451 · www.hayhouse.co.uk

Published and distributed in the Republic of South Africa by: Hay House SA (Pty), Ltd.,
P.O. Box 990, Witkoppen 2068 · Phone/Fax: 27-11-467-8904 · www.hayhouse.co.za

Published in India by: Hay House Publishers India, Muskaan Complex, Plot No. 3, B-2, Vasant Kunj,
New Delhi 110 070 · Phone: 91-11-4176-1620 · Fax: 91-11-4176-1630 · www.hayhouse.co.in

Distributed in Canada by: Raincoast Books, 2440 Viking Way, Richmond, B.C. V6V 1N2 ·
Phone: 1-800-663-5714 · Fax: 1-800-565-3770 · www.raincoast.com